THIS BOOK BELONGS TO

Icon Publishing Limited
P. O. Box OD 972
Odorkor, Accra
Ghana
www.facebook.com/myicongh
www.twitter.com/myicongh
+233 (0)23 3505 055,

iconpublishingltd@gmail.com
iconpublishing@ymail.com
enquiries.icongh@gmail.com

Cover and Interior Design by iCON-gh +233 24 4890 432

ISBN: 978-9988-8566-0-1

ANIMALS IN THE MIDST OF FAMINE

A NIGERIAN FOLKTALE

Dan Odei

Kwame Insaidoo

This Nigerian folktale shows the trickery of the dog—and how he deceives all the animals in a terrible way during a serious famine.

Long, long ago, in the heart of the thickest forest in the animal kingdom, there was a horrible famine among all the animals. They all grew lean because they had nothing to eat. The lion could not bear the pangs of hunger anymore, so he called all the animals together to discuss how to get the food they needed to end the famine in their land.

The lion began by recounting the fact that such horrible hunger had never occurred in their land since the time he was born, so they should find every possible method to end the famine and ensure that every one of the animals had plenty of food to eat. The lion asked all the animals to bring good suggestions they could implement to end the famine in their land.

The dog suggested that since their mothers were old and near to death anyway, it was better to spare them the long agony of waiting for the inevitability of death. Instead they should kill all their mothers and eat them on daily basis until the famine ended. The dog insisted that since every animal had a mother, there would be plenty of meat to eat, and everyone would be full every day and would have no need for food from anywhere else.

The elephant agreed with the dog's suggestion and volunteered to kill his mother first because she was quite old and fat and her meat would be enough to last all the animals for at least one week. Since the lion was the leader of the pack, he suggested that they put the dog's idea to a vote.

The lion asked, "Do all of you agree to the dog's suggestion that we kill and eat our aging mothers?"

The animals burst into a chorus, "Yes, yes, yes, the dog is right. We shall eat our mothers."

The elephant did as he had promised and killed his big, aging mother first, and there was a big feast in the kingdom for all the hungry animals. They ate for several days, enjoying the delicious meat of the elephant.

Meanwhile, the dog, who had been the one to bring up the idea of killing their mothers, secretly hid his mother in a deep, dark cave in the middle of the jungle so she would not be killed. He said to her, "Mother, I think you'll be safe here," and his mother

A meeting of all animals convened by the Lion

sarcastically retorted, "If you don't turn back to kill me yourself, then I will be alright."

The dog sadly responded, "Oh, you are my sweet mother, and I will never kill you for a meal or anything else. The thought of killing you makes me sick to my stomach. And, by the way, only foolish and stupid animals kill their mothers for a meal—I will never consent to such an absurd idea."

The dog's mother responded that she was glad to have such a sensible son who loved his mother. Before the dog left to join the rest of the animals, he instructed his mother never to come out, but to stay in the cave and take care of all the meat he would be bringing to her. He left a large chunk of the elephant mother's meat for her, advising her to eat some and save some for rainy days.

When the dog joined the pack of animals the next day, they had already killed the lion's mother and were enjoying her meat, while laughing and singing to God about the bountiful harvest of meat in their kingdom. The dog joined the pack and ate the meat to his satisfaction. When the animals finished eating, they all fell asleep.

The dog made sure that all the animals were sound asleep, and then he slowly sneaked a large chunk of the day's meat and dragged it to the cave for his mother. This became a routine as the dog sneaked all kinds of meat into the dark cave for his mother, and the cave became full of all kinds of meat. The dog's mother took pains to dry and preserve all the meat left unused to ensure that it did not decay. She was extremely grateful to her son for providing all the meat she could possibly eat and allowing her to escape the terrible hunger. Unlike other mothers, she had also escaped a senseless death because she had a sensible son.

Finally, the dog's turn came to kill his mother. The clever dog went into the cave and looked through all the chunks of meat and took out large ones that were on the verge of spoiling. Then he brought them to the gathering of the animals.

The dog announced to the animals, "Here is the meat of my dear mother whom I killed yesterday because she was terribly sick and deathly afraid of being killed. It made her temporarily insane, which made her urinate all over the place; so, if you find that her meat is not as tasty as it should be, it was because her

The dog and his mother enjoying large chunks of the day's meet

temporary insanity made her blood run wildly throughout her body, which has affected the quality of her meat."

The lion thanked the dog for killing his mother and said, "We are grateful to you for bringing this idea of killing our mothers to end this horrible famine. You have made it possible for us to have plenty to eat, and so we shall continue to adore you for your intelligence, leadership, wisdom, and dedication to us."

The animals began to eat what they thought was the dog's mother's meat, and as they were eating, the rabbit said to the tortoise, "So, the dog's meat also tastes and smells like elephant."

The rabbit responded, "Sometimes the dog's meat can smell like the elephant's." The tortoise, equally worried, added that he smelled a rat. He believed something funny was going on because the meat he was eating was definitely not that of a dog.

The tortoise and the rabbit concluded that the dog's mother must still be alive and that they should jointly observe the dog's activities to see what they could find out. After eating what was allegedly the meat of the dog's mother, all the animals thanked the dog for his generosity. The routine of killing their mothers continued, and all the animals continued to have plenty of food to eat every day.

When all the animals had killed and eaten their mothers, the famine was still not over. In fact, scarcely had they finished eating all their mothers when the famine intensified. So, the dog's solution turned out to be only a temporary stopgap measure, and moreover the animals did not have sense enough to save any of the meat. They were greedy and foolhardy and had eaten it all after every killing.

The animals had grown lean and hungry again and were desperately looking for new methods of getting food. In the midst of this terrible hunger, the dog continued to look nice and fat, well groomed and beautiful, despite the fact that all the other animals were becoming thinner by the day. The clever and sensible dog had saved large chunks of the meat in the cave with his mother, so he had enough meat to last him many moons. Every night he sneaked into the cave to eat with his mother, and they laughed at the stupidity of the animals who had killed and eaten their mothers, and now had no mothers and nothing to eat.

The animals became suspicious of the dog's activities, so the lion selected the tortoise to keep an eye on the dog to find out why he was still looking good in the middle of the famine. The tortoise spied on the dog for more than a month and was about to give up his spying, when something piqued his interest. He kept vigil past midnight and saw the dog slowly and cautiously creeping into a deep, dark cave. The tortoise followed noiselessly till he reached the entrance of the cave and saw the dog's mother alive and well.

The tortoise angrily screamed at the dog, "You have betrayed us by your lies, wickedness, and selfishness!"

The dog agreed with the tortoise that he had been a little selfish and cautious, so he motioned for the tortoise to enter into the cave to see more of the meat. Once in the cave, the dog showed him all sorts of meat from the elephant, tiger, lion, hippopotamus, hyena, and others.

The dog whispered into his ear, "Friend, you see all kinds of meat here in the midst of this terrible famine .... You can either secretly join me, or you can announce it to all the animals who will push you aside and greedily consume the meat in a day—after that we would all continue to be hungry."

The dog asked the tortoise to sit down and eat as much meat as he could before they continued with their conversation. The tortoise sat down and ate as much meat as he could and promised the dog that he would not mention the incident to any of the other animals. The dog told the tortoise to secretly come to the cave at midnight every night to eat as much meat as he possibly could. The only condition was that he must keep their discussion secret and not to breathe a word of it to any of the other animals.

When the tortoise returned to the gathering of the anxious and curious animals who were waiting expectantly for his response, he said to them, "My fellow animals, it is always easy for us to cast suspicious glances at our fellow animals who are successful and hardworking; we tend to believe that they are duping all of us to become successful, but upon my vigorous investigation I found out that the dog loves all of us and would not do anything to hurt any of us. He looks good because he works with his mind, and you know something, brothers? Sometimes it is not only hard work that brings us fortune, but working smart—and that is the secret between the dog and many of us. The dog is innocent; he is not doing anything funny. But he taught me one lesson about worrying. He taught me that the more we worry about the famine, the thinner we will become. But when we refrain from worrying, we will grow just like the dog."

Many of the animals praised the tortoise for giving them good advice; but some, like the rabbit, thought the tortoise was delivering a lot of nonsense and lies to this gathering of his brethren. It sounded like one of the biggest lies the rabbit had ever heard.

Curiously enough, the tortoise began to grow large and beautiful despite the famine, and in about a month's time he had grown to twice his original size, which made all the animals suspicious of him and the dog once more. The lion selected the rabbit to find out what was making both the tortoise and the dog grow nice in the midst of the horrible famine in their land.

The rabbit spent a week watching the movements of both the dog and the tortoise to find out what funny business they were into, but he found out nothing. In the middle of the following week, toward midnight, the rabbit saw the dog and the tortoise whispering to each other, so the rabbit kept his keen eyes on them. To his amazement he saw that these two partners in crime were moving slowly and gingerly toward the entrance of what seemed to the rabbit to be a big hole.

The rabbit moved slowly behind them until he saw them enter into a cave. He followed them in and discovered all sorts of meat and the fact that the dog's mother was still alive. He was flabbergasted, dismayed, and shocked when he realized the brazen lies both the tortoise and the dog had been telling. He was particularly taken aback and felt nauseated upon remembering that it was the dog who had suggested that all the animals kill their mothers. He called them betrayers of the animal kingdom and promised to ensure that both the lion and elephant knew about the treachery of both animals.

The dog and tortoise calmed the rabbit down and asked him to look around the entire cave before he overreacted. As the rabbit looked around, he was appalled to see all kinds of meat piled in the cave, and as hungry as he was, he asked the dog and the tortoise to allow him to have something to eat. They told him that he could eat all the meat he possibly could, so the rabbit sat down and ate till he could not move. The dog assured him that he was lucky to be a member of their exclusive gentleman's club, with access to all this meat on daily basis and that he would be a fool to inform the rest of the hungry and starving animals about his good fortune.

The tortoise added that if he were to become such a fool and inform the rest of the animals, the other animals would eat all the meat in a day, and then they would all begin starving again.

The dog added, "In this world you have to be selfish to succeed. Indeed, each one must be for himself, so you, Rabbit, out of your own self interest, must join this exclusive club."

The rabbit accepted their purported wisdom and their invitation and decided to join their exclusive club, making them the gang of three wise animals. The rabbit joined the group and began eating as much meat as he could on daily basis; so, even though the famine persisted for a long time, the emaciated rabbit began to gain his weight back. Indeed he looked like he was getting nutritious meals on a daily basis.

The rabbit promising to report the treachery of both animals

All the animals complained bitterly to the lion to do something about the gang of three animals, because they just knew they were up to something funny; and so, unbeknownst to the three animals, the lion began watching them. One midnight, the lion followed cautiously, and in his usual hunting mode crept noiselessly behind the gang of three until he saw them enter a cave.

The lion also entered the cave and roared at them, "At long last, all your trickery and lies are over!"

He felt horribly deceived by the three little animals, and in his anger he seized the dog's mother and ate her at once. He called all the animals to the cave and ordered them to eat all the meat they could to their satisfaction, and he ate the rabbit, the tortoise, and the dog for their treachery. He advised all the animals to find new ways of living and to learn to develop their land; but he reminded them to eschew selfishness, lies, and cheating others, because those traits could lead to their own destruction.

The gang of three pleading for mercy from the Lion and other animals

Moral Lessons

This story raises important moral questions for all of us: Was the dog a good friend of the animals? How could he have deceived all of them by suggesting that they kill their mothers, but saved his own? A friend should watch our backs and stand by us in times of need, but did the dog do that? The tortoise and rabbit were not good friends of the animals either, as they deceived them and betrayed them for food. It is equally important to know that a sincere and true friend will never tell you to kill your mother—or anybody for that matter—or do something that will get you in trouble. By this standard, was the dog a true friend of the animals? With "friends" like the dog, tortoise, and rabbit, the animals didn't need enemies.

The story also cautions us to pay attention to the activities of our leaders when we are working together in a group. Had the animals paid attention, they would have discovered that the dog, tortoise, and rabbit were merely playing games and deceiving all the animals.

Answer the following questions:

1. a) Why did the Lion call all animals together?
   b) What did he tell them?
2. a) What was the dog's suggestion?
   b) Was it agreed after the votes were cast?
3. a) What did the dog do with his mother thereafter?
   b) What did she do with all the meat her son smuggled into the cave on daily basis?
4. a) What moved the tortoise and rabbit to suspect foulplay by the dog?
   b) Why didn't they reveal the dog's secret to all the animals?
5. a) Who caught and prompted the others about the selfish animals?
   b) What did he do to the dog's mother?
6. What have you learned from this folktale?
7. Find the meaning of the following words in the dictionary and use them in sentences of your own,
   i. Famine
   ii. Pangs
   iii. Implement
   iv. Agony

v. Inevitability

vi. Sarcastically

vii. Consent

viii. Absurd

ix. Chunk

x. Bountiful

xi. Allegedly

xii. Generosity

xiii. Intensified

xiv. Stopgap

xv. Spies

xvi. Piqued

xvii. Vigil

xviii. Vigorous

xix. Gingerly

xx. Flabbergasted

xxi. Dismayed

xxii. Bbrazen

xxiii. Nauseated

xxiv. Treachery

xxv. Purported

xxvi. Emaciated

xxvii. Eschew

8. What does the expression "He was particularly taken aback" mean?

9. The story conveys a sense of
    a. fear and fright
    b. deceit and betrayal
    c. work and happiness
    d. commitment

Answer the questions here.